COLLECTED ANIMAL POEMS

Ted Hughes

COLLECTED ANIMAL POEMS

VOLUME 4

The Thought-Fox

faber and faber
LONDON · BOSTON

First published in Great Britain in 1995
by Faber and Faber Limited
3 Queen Square London WC1N 3AU

Phototypeset by Wilmaset Ltd, Birkenhead, Wirral
Printed in England by MPG Books Ltd, Bodmin, Cornwall

This collection © Ted Hughes, 1995

Ted Hughes is hereby identified as author of this
work in accordance with section 77 of the Copyright,
Designs and Patents Act 1988

A CIP record for this book
is available from the British Library

ISBN 0–571–17627–5 (cased)
     0–571–17628–3 (pbk)

10 9 8 7 6 5 4 3

to Olwyn and Gerald

Contents

Wodwo

What am I? Nosing here, turning leaves over
Following a faint stain on the air to the river's edge
I enter water. What am I to split
The glassy grain of water looking upward I see the bed
Of the river above me upside down very clear
What am I doing here in mid-air? Why do I find
this frog so interesting as I inspect its most secret
interior and make it my own? Do these weeds
know me and name me to each other have they
seen me before, do I fit in their world? I seem
separate from the ground and not rooted but dropped
out of nothing casually I've no threads
fastening me to anything I can go anywhere
I seem to have been given the freedom
of this place what am I then? And picking
bits of bark off this rotten stump gives me
no pleasure and it's no use so why do I do it
me and doing that have coincided very queerly
But what shall I be called am I the first
have I an owner what shape am I what
shape am I am I huge if I go
to the end on this way past these trees and past these
    trees
till I get tired that's touching one wall of me
for the moment if I sit still how everything
stops to watch me I suppose I am the exact centre
but there's all this what is it roots
roots roots roots and here's the water
again very queer but I'll go on looking

Wolfwatching

Woolly-bear white, the old wolf
Is listening to London. His eyes, withered in
Under the white wool, black peepers,
While he makes nudging, sniffing offers
At the horizon of noise, the blue-cold April
Invitation of airs. The lump of meat
Is his confinement. He has probably had all his life
Behind wires, fraying his eye-efforts
On the criss-cross embargo. He yawns
Peevishly like an old man and the yawn goes
Right back into Kensington and there stops
Floored with glaze. Eyes
Have worn him away. Children's gazings
Have tattered him to a lumpish
Comfort of woolly play-wolf. He's weary.
He curls on the cooling stone
That gets heavier. Then again the burden
Of a new curiosity, a new testing
Of new noises, new people with new colours
Are coming in at the gate. He lifts
The useless weight and lets it sink back,
Stirring and settling in a ball of unease.
All his power is a tangle of old ends,
A jumble of leftover scraps and bits of energy
And bitten-off impulses and dismantled intuitions.
He can't settle. He's ruffling
And re-organizing his position all day
Like a sleepless half-sleep of growing agonies
In a freezing car. The day won't pass.
The night will be worse. He's waiting
For the anaesthetic to work

That has already taken his strength, his beauty
And his life.

He levers his stiffness erect
And angles a few tottering steps
Into his habits. He goes down to water
And drinks. Age is thirsty. Water
Just might help and ease. What else
Is there to do? He tries to find again
That warm position he had. He cowers
His hind legs to curl under him. Subsides
In a trembling of wolf-pelt he no longer
Knows how to live up to.
                       And here
Is a young wolf, still intact.
He knows how to lie, with his head,
The Asiatic eyes, the gunsights
Aligned effortless in the beam of his power.
He closes his pale eyes and is easy,
Bored easy. His big limbs
Are full of easy time. He's waiting
For the chance to live, then he'll be off.
Meanwhile the fence, and the shadow-flutter
Of moving people, and the roller-coaster
Roar of London surrounding, are temporary,
And cost him nothing, and he can afford
To prick his ears to all that and find nothing
As to forest. He still has the starlings
To amuse him. The scorched ancestries,
Grizzled into his back, are his royalty.
The rufous ears and neck are always ready.
He flops his heavy running paws, resplays them
On pebbles, and rests the huge engine

Of his purring head. A wolf
Dropped perfect on pebbles. For eyes
To put on a pedestal. A product
Without a market.
                    But all the time
The awful thing is happening: the iron inheritance,
The incredibly rich will, torn up
In neurotic boredom and eaten,
Now indigestible. All that restlessness
And lifting of ears, and aiming, and re-aiming
Of nose, is like a trembling
Of nervous breakdown, afflicted by voices.
Is he hearing the deer? Is he listening
To gossip of non-existent forest? Pestered
By the hour-glass panic of lemmings
Dwindling out of reach? He's run a long way
Now to find nothing and be patient.
Patience is suffocating in all those folds
Of deep fur. The fairy tales
Grow stale all around him
And go back into pebbles. His eyes
Keep telling him all this is real
And that he's a wolf – of all things
To be in the middle of London, of all
Futile, hopeless things. Do Arctics
Whisper on their wave-lengths – fantasy-draughts
Of escape and freedom? His feet,
The power-tools, lie in front of him –
He doesn't know how to use them. Sudden
Dramatic lift and re-alignment
Of his purposeful body –
                              the Keeper
Has come to freshen the water.

[4]

And the prodigious journeys
Are thrown down again in his
Loose heaps of rope.
The future's snapped and coiled back
Into a tangled lump, a whacking blow
That's damaged his brain. Quiet,
Amiable in his dogginess,
Disillusioned – all that preparation
Souring in his skin. His every yawn
Is another dose of poison. His every frolic
Releases a whole flood
Of new hopelessness which he then
Has to burn up in sleep. A million miles
Knotted in his paws. Ten million years
Broken between his teeth. A world
Stinking on the bone, pecked by sparrows.

He's hanging
Upside down on the wire
Of non-participation.
He's a tarot card, and he knows it.
He can howl all night
And dawn will pick up the same card
And see him painted on it, with eyes
Like doorframes in a desert
Between nothing and nothing.

The Bear

In the huge, wide-open, sleeping eye of the mountain
The bear is the gleam in the pupil
Ready to awake
And instantly focus.

The bear is glueing
Beginning to end
With glue from people's bones
In his sleep.

The bear is digging
In his sleep
Through the wall of the Universe
With a man's femur.

The bear is a well
Too deep to glitter
Where your shout
Is being digested.

The bear is a river
Where people bending to drink
See their dead selves.

The bear sleeps
In a kingdom of walls
In a web of rivers.

He is the ferryman
To dead land.

His price is everything.

Gnat-Psalm

'The Gnat is of more ancient lineage than man.'
HEBREW PROVERB

When the gnats dance at evening
Scribbling on the air, sparring sparely,
Scrambling their crazy lexicon,
Shuffling their dumb Cabala,
Under leaf shadow

Leaves only leaves
Between them and the broad swipes of the sun
Leaves muffling the dusty stabs of the late sun
From their frail eyes and crepuscular temperaments

Dancing
Dancing
Writing on the air, rubbing out everything they write
Jerking their letters into knots, into tangles
Everybody everybody else's yo-yo

Immense magnets fighting around a centre

Not writing and not fighting but singing
That the cycles of this Universe are no matter
That they are not afraid of the sun
That the one sun is too near
It blasts their song, which is of all the suns
That they are their own sun
Their own brimming over
At large in the nothing
Their wings blurring the blaze
Singing

[7]

That they are the nails
In the dancing hands and feet of the gnat-god
That they hear the wind suffering
Through the grass
And the evening tree suffering

The wind bowing with long cat-gut cries
And the long roads of dust
Dancing in the wind
The wind's dance, the death-dance, entering the
    mountain
And the cow-dung villages huddling to dust

But not the gnats, their agility
Has outleapt that threshold
And hangs them a little above the claws of the grass
Dancing
Dancing
In the glove shadows of the sycamore

A dance never to be altered
A dance giving their bodies to be burned

And their mummy faces will never be used

Their little bearded faces
Weaving and bobbing on the nothing
Shaken in the air, shaken, shaken
And their feet dangling like the feet of victims

O little Hasids
Ridden to death by your own bodies
Riding your bodies to death
You are the angels of the only heaven!
And God is an Almighty Gnat!
You are the greatest of all the galaxies!

My hands fly in the air, they are follies
My tongue hangs up in the leaves
My thoughts have crept into crannies

Your dancing

Your dancing

Rolls my staring skull slowly away into outer space.

And the Falcon Came

The gunmetal feathers
Of would not be put aside, would not falter.

The wing-knuckles
Of dividing the mountain, of hurling the world away
   behind him.

With the bullet-brow
Of burying himself head-first and ahead
Of his delicate bones, into the target
Collision.

The talons
Of a first, last, single blow
Of grasping complete the crux of rays.

With the tooled bill
Of plucking out the ghost
And feeding it to his eye-flame.

Of stripping down the loose, hot flutter of earth
To its component parts
For the reconstitution of Falcon.

With the eye
Of explosion of Falcon.

The Skylark Came

With its effort hooked to the sun, a swinging ladder

With its song
A labour of its whole body
Thatching the sun with bird-joy

To keep off the rains of weariness
The snows of extinction

With its labour
Of a useless excess, lifting what can only fall

With its crest
Which it intends to put on the sun

Which it meanwhile wears itself
So earth can be crested

With its song
Erected between dark and dark

The lark that lives and dies
In the service of its crest.

The Wild Duck

                                              got up with a cry
Shook off her Arctic swaddling

Pitched from the tower of the North Wind
And came spanking across water

The wild duck, fracturing egg-zero,
Left her mother the snow in her shawl of stars
Abandoned her father the black wind in his beard of
   stars

Got up out of the ooze before dawn

Now hangs her whispering arrival
Between earth-glitter and heaven-glitter

Calling softly to the fixed lakes

As earth gets up in the frosty dark, at the back of the
   Pole Star
And flies into dew
Through the precarious crack of light

Quacking Wake Wake

The Swift Comes the Swift

Casts aside the two-arm two-leg article –
The pain instrument
Flesh and soft entrails and nerves, and is off.

Hurls itself as if again beyond where it fell among roofs
Out through the lightning-split in the great oak of light

One wing below mineral limit
One wing above dream and number

Shears between life and death

Whiskery snarl-gape already gone ahead
The eyes in possession ahead

Screams guess its trajectory
Meteorite puncturing the veils of worlds

Whipcrack, the ear's glimpse
Is the smudge it leaves

Hunting the winged mote of death into the sun's retina
Picking the nymph of life
Off the mirror of the lake of atoms

Till the Swift
Who falls out of the blindness, swims up
From the molten, rejoins itself

Shadow to shadow – resumes proof, nests
Papery ashes
Of the uncontainable burning.

The Unknown Wren

Hidden in Wren, sings only Wren. He sings
World-proof Wren
In thunderlight, at wrestling daybreak. Wren unalterable
In the wind-buffed wood.

Wren is here, but nearly out of control –
A blur of throbbings –
Electrocution by the god of wrens –
A battle-frenzy, a transfiguration –

Wren is singing in the wet bush.
His song sings him, every feather is a tongue
He is a song-ball of tongues –
The head squatted back, the pin-beak stretching to swallow
    the sky

And the wings quiver-lifting, as in death-rapture,
Every feather a wing beating,
Wren is singing Wren – Wren of Wrens!
While his feet knot to a twig.

Imminent death only makes the wren more Wren-like
As harder sunlight, and realler earth-light.
Wren reigns! Wren is in power!
Under his upstart tail.

And when Wren sleeps even the star-drape heavens are a
    dream
Earth is just a bowl of ideas.

But now the lifted sun and the drenched woods rejoice
    with trembling –

WREN OF WRENS!

And Owl

Floats. A masked soul listening for death.
Death listening for a soul.
Small mouths and their incriminations are suspended.
Only the centre moves.

Constellations stand in awe. And the trees very still, the
    fields very still
As the Owl becalms deeper
To stillness.
Two eyes, fixed in the heart of heaven.

Nothing is neglected, in the Owl's stare.
The womb opens and the cry comes
And the shadow of the creature
Circumscribes its fate. And the Owl

Screams, again ripping the bandages off
Because of the shape of its throat, as if it were a torture
Because of the shape of its face, as if it were a prison
Because of the shape of its talons, as if they were
    inescapable

Heaven screams. Earth screams. Heaven eats. Earth is
    eaten.

And earth eats and heaven is eaten.

The Dove Came

Her breast big with rainbows
She was knocked down

The dove came, her wings clapped lightning
That scattered like twigs
She was knocked down

The dove came, her voice of thunder
A piling heaven of silver and violet
She was knocked down

She gave the flesh of her breast, and they ate her
She gave the milk of her blood, they drank her

The dove came again, a sun-blinding

And ear could no longer hear

Mouth was a disembowelled bird
Where the tongue tried to stir like a heart

And the dove alit
In the body of thorns.

Now deep in the dense body of thorns
A soft thunder
Nests her rainbows.

Gog

I woke to a shout: 'I am Alpha and Omega.'
Rocks and a few trees trembled
Deep in their own country.
I ran and an absence bounded beside me.

The dog's god is a scrap dropped from the table.
The mouse's saviour is a ripe wheat grain.
Hearing the Messiah cry
My mouth widens in adoration.

How fat are the lichens!
They cushion themselves on the silence.
The air wants for nothing.
The dust, too, is replete.

What was my error? My skull has sealed it out.
My great bones are massed in me.
They pound on the earth, my song excites them.
I do not look at the rocks and trees, I am frightened of
    what they see.

I listen to the song jarring my mouth
Where the skull-rooted teeth are in possession.
I am massive on earth. My feetbones beat on the earth
Over the sounds of motherly weeping . . .

Afterwards I drink at a pool quietly.
The horizon bears the rocks and trees away into twilight.
I lie down. I become darkness.

Darkness that all night sings and circles stamping.

The Gulkana

Jumbled iceberg hills, away to the north –
And a long wreath of fire-haze.

The Gulkana, where it meets the Copper,
Swung, jade, out of the black spruce forest,
And disappeared into it.

Strange word, Gulkana. What does it mean?
A pre-Columbian glyph.
A pale blue thread – scrawled with a child's hand
Across our map. A Lazarus of water
Returning from seventy below.
                                  We stumbled,
Not properly awake,
In a weird light – a bombardment
Of purplish emptiness –
Among phrases that lumped out backwards. Among
    rocks
That kept startling me – too rock-like,
Hypnagogic rocks –
                        A scrapyard of boxy shacks
And supermarket refuse, dogs, wrecked pick-ups,
The Indian village where we bought our pass
Was comatose – on the stagnation toxins
Of a cultural vasectomy. They were relapsing
To Cloud-like-a-Boulder, Mica, Bear, Magpie.

We hobbled along a tightrope shore of pebbles
Under a trickling bluff
That bounced the odd pebble onto us, eerily.
(The whole land in perpetual seismic tremor.)
Gulkana –

Biblical, a deranging cry
From the wilderness, burst past us.
A stone voice that dragged at us.
I found myself clinging
To the lifted skyline fringe of rag spruce
And the subsidence under my bootsoles
With balancing glances – nearly a fear,
Something I kept trying to deny

With deliberate steps. But it came with me
As if it swayed on my pack –
A nape-of-the-neck unease. We'd sploshed far enough
Through the spongy sinks of the permafrost
For this river's
Miraculous fossils – creatures that each midsummer
Resurrected through it, in a blood-rich flesh.
Pilgrims for a fish!
Prospectors for the lode in a fish's eye!

In that mercury light
My illusion developed. I felt hunted.
I tested my fear. It seemed to live in my neck –
A craven, bird-headed alertness.
And in my eye
That felt blind somehow to what I stared at
As if it stared at me. And in my ear –
So wary for the air-stir in the spruce-tips
My ear-drum almost ached. I explained it
To my quietly arguing, lucid panic
As my fear of one inside me,
A bodiless twin, some doppelgänger
Disinherited other, unliving,
Ever-living, a larva from prehistory,
Whose journey this was, who now exulted

Recognizing his home,
And whose gaze I could feel as he watched me
Fiddling with my gear – the interloper,
The fool he had always hated. We pitched our tent

And for three days
Our tackle scratched the windows of the express torrent.

We seemed underpowered. Whatever we hooked
Bent in air, a small porpoise,
Then went straight downriver under the weight
And joined the glacial landslide of the Copper
Which was the colour of cement.

Even when we got one ashore
It was too big to eat.

But there was the eye!
                          I peered into that lens
Seeking what I had come for. (What had I come for?
The camera-flash? The burned-out, ogling bulb?)
What I saw was small, crazed, snake-like.
It made me think of a dwarf, shrunken sun
And of the black, refrigerating pressures
Under the Bering Sea.

We relaunched their mulberry-dark torsos,
Those gulping, sooted mouths, the glassy visors –

Arks of an undelivered covenant,
Egg-sacs of their own Eden,
Seraphs of heavy ore

They surged away, magnetized,
Into the furnace boom of the Gulkana.

Bliss had fixed their eyes
Like an anaesthetic. They were possessed
By that voice in the river
And its accompaniment –
The flutes, the drumming. And they rose and sank
Like voices, themselves like singers
In its volume. We watched them, deepening away.
They looked like what they were – somnambulists,
Drugged, ritual victims, melting away
Towards a sacrament –

a consummation

That could only be death.
Which it would be, within some numbered days,
On some stony platform of water,
In a spillway, where a man could hardly stand –
Aboriginal Americans,
High among rains, in an opening of the hills,
They will begin to circle,
Shedding their ornaments,
In shufflings and shudders, male by female,
Begin to dance their deaths –
The current hosing over their brows and shoulders,
Bellies riven open and shaken empty
Into a gutter of pebbles
In the orgy of eggs and sperm,
The dance orgy of being reborn
From which masks and regalia drift empty,
Torn off – at last their very bodies,
In the numbed, languorous frenzy, as obstacles,
Ripped away –

ecstasy dissolving

In the mercy of water, at the star of the source,
Devoured by revelation,

Every molecule drained, and counted, and healed
Into the amethyst of emptiness –

I came back to myself. A spectre of fragments
Lifted my quivering coffee, in the aircraft,
And sipped at it.
I imagined the whole 747
As if a small boy held it
Making its noise. A spectre,
Escaping the film's flicker, peered from the porthole
Under the sun's cobalt core-darkness
Down at Greenland's corpse
Tight-sheeted with snow-glare.
                              Word by word
The voice of the river moved in me.
It was like lovesickness.
A numbness, a secret bleeding.
Waking in my body.
                      Telling of the King
Salmon's eye.
                    Of the blood-mote mosquito.

And the stilt-legged, subarctic, one-rose rose
With its mock aperture
Tilting toward us
In our tent doorway, its needle tremor.

And the old Indian Headman, in his tatty jeans and
        socks, who smiled
Adjusting to our incomprehension – his face
A whole bat, that glistened and stirred.

Song of a Rat

I   THE RAT'S DANCE

The rat is in the trap, it is in the trap,
And attacking heaven and earth with a mouthful of
　　screeches like torn tin,

An effective gag.
When it stops screeching, it pants

And cannot think
'This has no face, it must be God' or

'No answer is also an answer.'
Iron jaws, strong as the whole earth

Are stealing its backbone
For a crumpling of the Universe with screechings,

For supplanting every human brain inside its skull with a
　　rat-body that knots and unknots,
A rat that goes on screeching,

Trying to uproot itself into each escaping screech,
But its long fangs bar that exit

The incisors bared to the night spaces, threatening the
　　constellations,
The glitterers in the black, to keep off,

Keep their distance,
While it works this out.

The rat understands suddenly. It bows and is still,
With a little beseeching of blood on its nose-end.

[23]

II THE RAT'S VISION

The rat hears the wind saying something in the straw
And the night-fields that have come up to the fence,
  leaning their silence,
The widowed land
With its trees that know how to cry

The rat sees the farm bulk of beam and stone
Wobbling like reflection on water.
The wind is pushing from the gulf
Through the old barbed wire, in through the trenched
  gateway,
  past the gates of the ear, deep into the worked design of
  days,

Breathes onto the solitary snow crystal

The rat screeches
And 'Do not go' cry the dandelions, from their heads of
  folly
And 'Do not go' cry the yard cinders, who have no
  future, only their infernal aftermath
And 'Do not go' cries the cracked trough by the gate,
  fatalist of starlight and zero

'Stay' says the arrangement of stars

Forcing the rat's head down into godhead.

III THE RAT'S FLIGHT

The heaven shudders, a flame unrolled like a whip,
And the stars jolt in their sockets.
And the sleep-souls of eggs
Wince under the shot of shadow –

That was the Shadow of the Rat
Crossing into power
Never to be buried

The horned Shadow of the Rat
Casting here by the door
A bloody gift for the dogs

While it supplants Hell.

View of a Pig

The pig lay on a barrow dead.
It weighed, they said, as much as three men.
Its eyes closed, pink-white eyelashes.
Its trotters stuck straight out.

Such weight and thick pink bulk
Set in death seemed not just dead.
It was less than lifeless, further off.
It was like a sack of wheat..

I thumped it without feeling remorse.
One feels guilty insulting the dead,
Walking on graves. But this pig
Did not seem able to accuse.

It was too dead. Just so much
A poundage of lard and pork.
Its last dignity had entirely gone.
It was not a figure of fun.

Too dead now to pity.
To remember its life, din, stronghold
Of earthly pleasure as it had been,
Seemed a false effort, and off the point.

Too deadly factual. Its weight
Oppressed me – how could it be moved?
And the trouble of cutting it up!
The gash in its throat was shocking, but not pathetic.

Once I ran at a fair in the noise
To catch a greased piglet
That was faster and nimbler than a cat;
Its squeal was the rending of metal.

Pigs must have hot blood, they feel like ovens.
Their bite is worse than a horse's –
They chop a half-moon clean out.
They eat cinders, dead cats.

Distinctions and admirations such
As this one was long finished with.
I stared at it a long time. They were going to scald it,
Scald it and scour it like a doorstep.

Pike

Pike, three inches long, perfect
Pike in all parts, green tigering the gold.
Killers from the egg: the malevolent aged grin.
They dance on the surface among the flies.

Or move, stunned by their own grandeur,
Over a bed of emerald, silhouette
Of submarine delicacy and horror.
A hundred feet long in their world.

In ponds, under the heat-struck lily pads –
Gloom of their stillness:
Logged on last year's black leaves, watching upwards.
Or hung in an amber cavern of weeds

The jaws' hooked clamp and fangs
Not to be changed at this date;
A life subdued to its instrument;
The gills kneading quietly, and the pectorals.

Three we kept behind glass,
Jungled in weed: three inches, four,
And four and a half: fed fry to them –
Suddenly there were two. Finally one.

With a sag belly and the grin it was born with.
And indeed they spare nobody.
Two, six pounds each, over two feet long,
High and dry and dead in the willow-herb –

One jammed past its gills down the other's gullet:
The outside eye stared: as a vice locks –
The same iron in this eye
Though its film shrank in death.

A pond I fished, fifty yards across,
Whose lilies and muscular tench
Had outlasted every visible stone
Of the monastery that planted them –

Stilled legendary depth:
It was as deep as England. It held
Pike too immense to stir, so immense and old
That past nightfall I dared not cast

But silently cast and fished
With the hair frozen on my head
For what might move, for what eye might move.
The still splashes on the dark pond,

Owls hushing the floating woods
Frail on my ear against the dream
Darkness beneath night's darkness had freed,
That rose slowly toward me, watching.

The Jaguar

The apes yawn and adore their fleas in the sun.
The parrots shriek as if they were on fire, or strut
Like cheap tarts to attract the stroller with the nut.
Fatigued with indolence, tiger and lion

Lie still as the sun. The boa constrictor's coil
Is a fossil. Cage after cage seems empty, or
Stinks of sleepers from the breathing straw.
It might be painted on a nursery wall.

But who runs like the rest past these arrives
At a cage where the crowd stands, stares, mesmerized,
As a child at a dream, at a jaguar hurrying enraged
Through prison darkness after the drills of his eyes

On a short fierce fuse. Not in boredom –
The eye satisfied to be blind in fire,
By the bang of blood in the brain deaf the ear –
He spins from the bars, but there's no cage to him

More than to the visionary his cell:
His stride is wildernesses of freedom:
The world rolls under the long thrust of his heel.
Over the cage floor the horizons come.

Hawk Roosting

I sit in the top of the wood, my eyes closed.
Inaction, no falsifying dream
Between my hooked head and hooked feet:
Or in sleep rehearse perfect kills and eat.

The convenience of the high trees!
The air's buoyancy and the sun's ray
Are of advantage to me;
And the earth's face upward for my inspection.

My feet are locked upon the rough bark.
It took the whole of Creation
To produce my foot, my each feather:
Now I hold Creation in my foot

Or fly up, and revolve it all slowly –
I kill where I please because it is all mine.
There is no sophistry in my body:
My manners are tearing off heads –

The allotment of death.
For the one path of my flight is direct
Through the bones of the living.
No arguments assert my right:

The sun is behind me.
Nothing has changed since I began.
My eye has permitted no change.
I am going to keep things like this.

The Horses

I climbed through woods in the hour-before-dawn dark.
Evil air, a frost-making stillness,

Not a leaf, not a bird –
A world cast in frost. I came out above the wood

Where my breath left tortuous statues in the iron light.
But the valleys were draining the darkness

Till the moorline – blackening dregs of the brightening
    grey –
Halved the sky ahead. And I saw the horses:

Huge in the dense grey – ten together –
Megalith-still. They breathed, making no move,

With draped manes and tilted hind-hooves,
Making no sound.

I passed: not one snorted or jerked its head.
Grey silent fragments

Of a grey silent world.

I listened in emptiness on the moor-ridge.
The curlew's tear turned its edge on the silence.

Slowly detail leafed from the darkness. Then the sun
Orange, red, red, erupted

Silently, and splitting to its core tore and flung cloud,
Shook the gulf open, showed blue,

And the big planets hanging.
I turned.

Stumbling in the fever of a dream, down toward
The dark woods, from the kindling tops,

And came to the horses.
                    There, still they stood,
But now steaming and glistening under the flow of light,

Their draped stone manes, their tilted hind-hooves
Stirring under a thaw while all around them

The frost showed its fires. But still they made no sound.
Not one snorted or stamped,

Their hung heads patient as the horizons,
High over valleys, in the red levelling rays –

In din of the crowded streets, going among the years, the
    faces,
May I still meet my memory in so lonely a place

Between the streams and the red clouds, hearing
    curlews,
Hearing the horizons endure.

The Merry Mink

                    – the Arctic Indian's
Black bagful of hunter's medicine –
Now has to shift for himself.

Since he's here, he's decided to like it.
Now it is my turn, he says,
To enjoy my pelt uselessly.

I am the Mighty Northern Night, he says,
In my folktale form.
See, I leave my stars at the river's brim.

Little Black Thundercloud, lost from his mythology,
A-boil with lightnings
He can't get rid of. He romps through the ramsons

(Each one like a constellation), topples into the river,
Jolly goblin, realist-optimist,
(Even his trapped, drowned snake-head grins)

As if he were deathless. Bobs up
Ruffed with a tough primeval glee. Crams trout, nine
    together,
Into his bank-hole – his freezer –

Where they rot in three days. Makes love
Eight hours at a go.
                    My doings and my pelt,
He says, are a Platonic idea

Where I live with God.

Bones

Bones is a crazy pony.
Moon-white – star-mad.
All skull and skeleton.

Her hooves pound. The sleeper awakes with a cry.

Who has broken her in?
Who has mounted her and come back
Or kept her?

She lifts under them, the snaking crest of a bullwhip.

Hero by hero they go –
Grimly get astride
And their hair lifts.

She laughs, smelling the battle – their cry comes back.

Who can live her life?
Every effort to hold her or turn her falls off her
Like rotten harness.

Their smashed faces come back, the wallets and the
    watches.

And this is the stunted foal of the earth –
She that kicks the cot
To flinders and is off.

Swifts

Fifteenth of May. Cherry blossom. The swifts
Materialize at the tip of a long scream
Of needle. 'Look! They're back! Look!' And they're gone
On a steep

Controlled scream of skid
Round the house-end and away under the cherries.
  Gone.
Suddenly flickering in sky summit, three or four
  together,
Gnat-whisp frail, and hover-searching, and listening

For air-chills – are they too early? With a bowing
Power-thrust to left, then to right, then a flicker they
Tilt into a slide, a tremble for balance,
Then a lashing down disappearance

Behind elms.
                    They've made it again
Which means the globe's still working, the Creation's
Still waking refreshed, our summer's
Still all to come –
                    And here they are, here they are
  again
Erupting across yard stones
Shrapnel-scatter terror. Frog-gapers,
Speedway goggles, international mobsters –

A bolas of three or four wire screams
Jockeying across each other
On their switchback wheel of death.
They swat past, hard-fletched,

Veer on the hard air, toss up over the roof,
And are gone again. Their mole-dark labouring,
Their lunatic limber scramming frenzy
And their whirling blades

Sparkle out into blue –
                              Not ours any more.
Rats ransacked their nests so now they shun us.
Round luckier houses now
They crowd their evening dirt-track meetings,

Racing their discords, screaming as if speed-burned,
Head-height, clipping the doorway
With their leaden velocity and their butterfly lightness,
Their too much power, their arrow-thwack into the
    eaves.

Every year a first-fling, nearly-flying
Misfit flopped in our yard,
Groggily somersaulting to get airborne.
He bat-crawled on his tiny useless feet, tangling his flails

Like a broken toy, and shrieking thinly
Till I tossed him up – then suddenly he flowed away
    under
His bowed shoulders of enormous swimming power,
Slid away along levels wobbling

On the fine wire they have reduced life to,
And crashed among the raspberries.
Then followed fiery hospital hours
In a kitchen. The moustached goblin savage

Nested in a scarf. The bright blank
Blind, like an angel, to my meat-crumbs and flies.
Then eyelids resting. Wasted clingers curled.
The inevitable balsa death.

                              Finally burial

For the husk
Of my little Apollo –

The charred scream
Folded in its huge power.

The Howling of Wolves

Is without world.

What are they dragging up and out on their long leashes of
    sound
That dissolve in the mid-air silence?

Then crying of a baby, in this forest of starving silences,
Brings the wolves running.
Tuning of a viola, in this forest delicate as an owl's ear,
Brings the wolves running – brings the steel traps clashing
    and slavering,
The steel furred to keep it from cracking in the cold,
The eyes that never learn how it has come about
That they must live like this,

That they must live

Innocence crept into minerals.

The wind sweeps through and the hunched wolf shivers.
It howls you cannot say whether out of agony or joy.

The earth is under its tongue,
A dead weight of darkness, trying to see through its eyes.
The wolf is living for the earth.
But the wolf is small, it comprehends little.

It goes to and fro, trailing its haunches and whimpering
    horribly.
It must feed its fur.

The night snows stars and the earth creaks.

Thrushes

Terrifying are the attent sleek thrushes on the lawn,
More coiled steel than living – a poised
Dark deadly eye, those delicate legs
Triggered to stirrings beyond sense – with a start, a bounce,
    a stab
Overtake the instant and drag out some writhing thing.
No indolent procrastinations and no yawning stares.
No sighs or head-scratchings. Nothing but bounce and
    stab
And a ravening second.

Is it their single-mind-sized skulls, or a trained
Body, or genius, or a nestful of brats
Gives their days this bullet and automatic
Purpose? Mozart's brain had it, and the shark's mouth
That hungers down the blood-smell even to a leak of its
    own
Side and devouring of itself: efficiency which
Strikes too streamlined for any doubt to pluck at it
Or obstruction deflect.

With a man it is otherwise. Heroisms on horseback,
Outstripping his desk-diary at a broad desk,
Carving at a tiny ivory ornament
For years: his act worships itself – while for him,
Though he bends to be blent in the prayer, how loud and
    above what
Furious spaces of fire do the distracting devils
Orgy and hosannah, under what wilderness
Of black silent waters weep.

An August Salmon

Upstream and downstream, the river's closed.
Summer wastes in the pools.
A sunken calendar unfurls,
Fruit ripening as the petals rot.

A holed-up gangster,
He dozes, his head on the same stone,
Gazing towards the skylight,
Waiting for time to run out on him.

Alone, in a cellar of ashroots,
The bridegroom, mortally wounded
By love and destiny,
Features deforming with deferment.

His beauty bleeding invisibly
From every lift of his gills.

He gulps, awkward in his ponderous regalia,
But his eye stays rapt,
Elephantine, Arctic –
A god, on earth for the first time,
With the clock of love and death in his body.

Four feet under weightless, premature leaf-crisps
Stuck in the sliding sky. Sometimes
A wind wags a bramble up there.

The pulsing tiny trout, so separately fated,
Glue themselves to the stones near him.

His tail-frond, the life-root,
Fondling the poor flow, stays him
Sleeked ice, a smear of being
Over his anchor shadow.

        Monkish, caressed
He kneels. He bows
Into the ceaseless gift
That unwinds the spool of his strength.

Dusk narrows too quickly. Manic depressive
Unspent, poltergeist anti-gravity
Spins him in his pit, levitates him
Through a fountain of plate glass,

Reveals his dragonized head,
The March-flank's ice-floe soul-flash
Rotted to a muddy net of bruise,
Flings his coil at the remainder of light –

Red-black and nearly unrecognizable,
He drops back, helpless with weight,
Tries to shake loose the riveted skull
And its ghoul decor –
                sinks to the bed
Of his wedding cell, the coma waiting
For execution and death
In the skirts of his bride.

Skylarks

I

The lark begins to go up
Like a warning
As if the globe were uneasy –

Barrel-chested for heights,
Like an Indian of the high Andes,

A whippet head, barbed like a hunting arrow,

But leaden
With muscle
For the struggle
Against
Earth's centre.

And leaden
For ballast
In the rocketing storms of the breath.

Leaden
Like a bullet
To supplant
Life from its centre.

II

Crueller than owl or eagle
A towered bird, shot through the crested head
With the command, Not die

But climb

Climb

Sing

Obedient as to death a dead thing.

III

I suppose you just gape and let your gaspings
Rip in and out through your voicebox
                              O lark

And sing inwards as well as outwards
Like a breaker of ocean milling the shingle
                              O lark

O song, incomprehensibly both ways –
Joy! Help! Joy! Help!
                  O lark

IV

You stop to rest, far up, you teeter
Over the drop

But not stopping singing

Resting only a second

Dropping just a little

Then up and up and up

Like a mouse with drowning fur
Bobbing and bobbing at the well-wall

Lamenting, mounting a little –

But the sun will not take notice
And the earth's centre smiles.

V

My idleness curdles
Seeing the lark labour near its cloud
Scrambling
In a nightmare difficulty
Up through the nothing

Its feathers thrash, its heart must be drumming like a
 motor,
As if it were too late, too late

Dithering in ether
Its song whirls faster and faster
And the sun whirls
The lark is evaporating
Till my eye's gossamer snaps,
        and my hearing floats back widely to earth

After which the sky lies blank open
Without wings, and the earth is a folded clod.

Only the sun goes silently and endlessly on with the lark's
 song.

VI

All the dreary Sunday morning
Heaven is a madhouse
With the voices and frenzies of the larks,

Squealing and gibbering and cursing

Heads flung back, as I see them,
Wings almost torn off backward – far up

Like sacrifices set floating
The cruel earth's offerings

The mad earth's missionaries.

VII

Like those flailing flames
That lift from the fling of a bonfire
Claws dangling full of what they feed on

The larks carry their tongues to the last atom
Battering and battering their last sparks out at the limit –
So it's a relief, a cool breeze
When they've had enough, when they're burned out
And the sun's sucked them empty
And the earth gives them the OK.

And they relax, drifting with changed notes

Dip and float, not quite sure if they may
Then they are sure and they stoop

And maybe the whole agony was for this

The plummeting dead drop

With long cutting screams buckling like razors

But just before they plunge into the earth

They flare and glide off low over grass, then up
To land on a wall-top, crest up,

Weightless,
Paid-up,
Alert,

Conscience perfect.

[46]

Tiger-Psalm

The tiger kills hungry. The machine guns
Talk, talk, talk across their Acropolis.
The tiger
Kills expertly, with anaesthetic hand.
The machine guns
Carry on arguing in heaven
Where numbers have no ears, where there is no blood.
The tiger
Kills frugally, after close inspection of the map.
The machine guns shake their heads,
They go on chattering statistics.
The tiger kills by thunderbolt:
God of her own salvation.
The machine guns
Proclaim the Absolute, according to Morse,
In a code of bangs and holes that make men frown.
The tiger
Kills with beautiful colours in her face,
Like a flower painted on a banner.
The machine guns
Are not interested.
They laugh. They are not interested. They speak and
Their tongues burn soul-blue, haloed with ashes,
Puncturing the illusion.
The tiger
Kills and licks her victim all over carefully.
The machine guns
Leave a crust of blood hanging on the nails
In an orchard of scrap iron.
The tiger
Kills

With the strength of five tigers, kills exalted.
The machine guns
Permit themselves a snigger. They eliminate the error
With a to-fro dialectic
And the point proved stop speaking.
The tiger
Kills like the fall of a cliff, one-sinewed with the earth,
Himalayas under eyelid, Ganges under fur –

Does not kill.

Does not kill. The tiger blesses with a fang.
The tiger does not kill but opens a path
Neither of Life nor of Death:
The tiger within the tiger:
The Tiger of the Earth.
                    O Tiger!
O Sister of the Viper!
                    O Beast in Blossom!

A Sparrow Hawk

Slips from your eye-corner – overtaking
Your first thought.

Through your mulling gaze over haphazard earth
The sun's cooled carbon wing
Whets the eye-beam.

Those eyes in their helmet
Still wired direct
To the nuclear core – they alone

Laser the lark-shaped hole
In the lark's song.

You find the fallen spurs, among soft ashes.

And maybe you find him

Materialized by twilight and dew
Still as a listener –

The warrior

Blue shoulder-cloak wrapped about him,
Leaning, hunched,
Among the oaks of the harp.

The Black Rhino

This is the Black Rhino, the elastic boulder, coming at a
	gallop.
The boulder with a molten core, the animal missile,
Enlarging towards you. This is him in his fame –

Whose past is Behemoth, sixty million years printing the
	strata
Whose present is the brain-blink behind a recoiling
	gunsight
Whose future is a cheap watch shaken in your ear

Listen – bedrock accompanies him, a drumbeat
But his shadow over the crisp tangle of grass-tips
	hesitates, passes, hesitates, passes lightly
As a moth at noon

For this is the Black Rhino, who vanishes as he
	approaches
Every second there is less and less of him
By the time he reaches you nothing will remain, maybe,
	but the horn – an ornament for a lady's lap

Quick, now, the light is perfect for colour – catch the
	wet, mud caul, compact of extinct forms, that protects
	his blood from the rays
Video the busy thirst of his hair-fringed ears drinking
	safety from the burnt air
Get a shot of his cocked tail carrying its own little torch
	of courageous whiskers

Zoom in on the lava peephole where prehistory peers
    from the roots of his horn
(Every moment more and more interested)
Get a close-up of his horn

Which is an electric shock to your bootsoles (you bowed
    over your camera), as if a buried thing burst from
    beneath you, as if he resurrected beneath you,
Erupting from dust and thorns,
At a horn-down gallop, the hieroglyph of amazement –

Quickly, quick, or even as you stare
He will have dissolved
Into a gagging stench, in the shimmer.

Bones will come out on the negative.

An Otter

Underwater eyes, an eel's
Oil of water body, neither fish nor beast is the otter:
  Four-legged yet water-gifted, to outfish fish;
    With webbed feet and long ruddering tail
    And a round head like an old tomcat.

  Brings the legend of himself
From before wars or burials, in spite of hounds and
                              vermin-poles;
  Does not take root like the badger. Wanders, cries;
    Gallops along land he no longer belongs to;
    Re-enters the water by melting.

  Of neither water nor land. Seeking
Some world lost when first he dived, that he cannot
                              come at since,
  Takes his changed body into the holes of lakes;
    As if blind, cleaves the stream's push till he licks
    The pebbles of the source; from sea

  To sea crosses in three nights
Like a king in hiding. Crying to the old shape of the
                              starlit land,
  Over sunken farms where the bats go round,
    Without answer. Till light and birdsong come
    Walloping up roads with the milk wagon.

The hunt's lost him. Pads on mud,
Among sedges, nostrils a surface bead,
The otter remains, hours. The air,
Circling the globe, tainted and necessary,

Mingling tobacco-smoke, hounds and parsley,
Comes carefully to the sunk lungs.
So the self under the eye lies,
Attendant and withdrawn. The otter belongs

In double robbery and concealment –
From water that nourishes and drowns, and from land
That gave him his length and the mouth of the hound.
He keeps fat in the limpid integument

Reflections live on. The heart beats thick,
Big trout muscle out of the dead cold;
Blood is the belly of logic; he will lick
The fishbone bare. And can take stolen hold

On a bitch otter in a field full
Of nervous horses, but linger nowhere.
Yanked above hounds, reverts to nothing at all,
To this long pelt over the back of a chair.

The Thought-Fox

I imagine this midnight moment's forest:
Something else is alive
Beside the clock's loneliness
And this blank page where my fingers move.

Through the window I see no star;
Something more near
Though deeper within darkness
Is entering the loneliness:

Cold, delicately as the dark snow
A fox's nose touches twig, leaf;
Two eyes serve a movement, that now
And again now, and now, and now

Sets neat prints into the snow
Between trees, and warily a lame
Shadow lags by stump and in hollow
Of a body that is bold to come

Across clearings, an eye,
A widening deepening greenness,
Brilliantly, concentratedly,
Coming about its own business

Till, with a sudden sharp hot stink of fox,
It enters the dark hole of the head.
The window is starless still; the clock ticks,
The page is printed.

Night Arrival of Sea-Trout

Honeysuckle hanging her fangs.
Foxglove rearing her open belly.
Dogrose touching the membrane.

Through the dew's mist, the oak's mass
Comes plunging, tossing dark antlers.

Then a shattering
Of the river's hole, where something leaps out –

An upside-down, buried heaven
Snarls, moon-mouthed, and shivers.

Summer dripping stars, biting at the nape.
Lobworms coupling in saliva.
Earth singing under her breath.

And out in the hard corn a horned god
Running and leaping
With a bat in his drum.

Second Glance at a Jaguar

Skinful of bowls, he bowls them,
The hip going in and out of joint, dropping the spine
With the urgency of his hurry
Like a cat going along under thrown stones, under cover,
Glancing sideways, running
Under his spine. A terrible, stump-legged waddle
Like a thick Aztec disemboweller,
Club-swinging, trying to grind some square
Socket between his hind legs round,
Carrying his head like a brazier of spilling embers,
And the black bit of his mouth, he takes it
Between his back teeth, he has to wear his skin out,
He swipes a lap at the water-trough as he turns,
Swivelling the ball of his heel on the polished spot,
Showing his belly like a butterfly,
At every stride he has to turn a corner
In himself and correct it. His head
Is like the worn-down stump of another whole jaguar,
His body is just the engine shoving it forward,
Lifting the air up and shoving on under,
The weight of his fangs hanging the mouth open,
Bottom jaw combing the ground. A gorged look,
Gangster, club-tail lumped along behind gracelessly,
He's wearing himself to heavy ovals,
Muttering some mantra, some drum-song of murder
To keep his rage brightening, making his skin
Intolerable, spurred by the rosettes, the Cain-brands,
Wearing the spots off from the inside,
Rounding some revenge. Going like a prayer-wheel,
The head dragging forward, the body keeping up,

The hind legs lagging. He coils, he flourishes
The blackjack tail as if looking for a target,
Hurrying through the underworld, soundless.

Little Whale Song

for Charles Causley

What do they think of themselves
With their global brains –
The tide-power voltage illumination
Of those brains? Their X-ray all-dimension

Grasp of this world's structures, their brains budded
Clone replicas of the electron world
Lit and re-imagining the world,
Perfectly tuned receivers and perceivers,

Each one a whole tremulous world
Feeling through the world? What
Do they make of each other?

'We are beautiful. We stir

Our self-colour in the pot of colours
Which is the world. At each
Tail-stroke we deepen
Our being into the world's lit substance,

And our joy into the world's
Spinning bliss, and our peace
Into the world's floating, plumed peace.'

Their body-tons, echo-chambered,

Amplify the whisper
Of current and airs, of sea-peoples
And planetary manoeuvres,
Of seasons, of shores, and of their own

Moon-lifted incantation, as they dance
Through the original Earth-drama
In which they perform, as from the beginning,
The Royal House.
                    The loftiest, spermiest

Passions, the most exquisite pleasures,
The noblest characters, the most god-like
Oceanic presence and poise –

The most terrible fall.

A Dove

Snaps its twig-tether – mounts –
Dream-yanked up into vacuum
Wings snickering.

Another, in a shatter, hurls dodging away up.

They career through tree-mazes –
Nearly uncontrollable love-weights.

Or now
Temple-dancers, possessed, and steered
By solemn powers
Through insane, stately convulsions.

Porpoises
Of dove-lust and blood splendour
With arcs
And plungings, and spray-slow explosions.

Now violently gone
Riding the snake of the long love-whip
Among flarings of mares and stallions

Now staying
Coiled on a bough
Bubbling molten, wobbling top-heavy
Into one and many.

An October Salmon

He's lying in poor water, a yard or so depth of poor
    safety,
Maybe only two feet under the no-protection of an
    outleaning small oak,
Half under a tangle of brambles.

After his two thousand miles, he rests,
Breathing in that lap of easy current
In his graveyard pool.

About six pounds weight,
Four years old at most, and hardly a winter at sea –
But already a veteran,
Already a death-patched hero. So quickly it's over!

So briefly he roamed the gallery of marvels!
Such sweet months, so richly embroidered into earth's
    beauty-dress,
Her life-robe –
Now worn out with her tirelessness, her insatiable quest,
Hangs in the flow, a frayed scarf –

An autumnal pod of his flower,
The mere hull of his prime, shrunk at shoulder and
    flank,

With the sea-going Aurora Borealis
Of his April power –
The primrose and violet of that first upfling in the
    estuary –
Ripened to muddy dregs,
The river reclaiming his sea-metals.

In the October light
He hangs there, patched with leper-cloths.

Death has already dressed him
In her clownish regimentals, her badges and decorations,
Mapping the completion of his service,
His face a ghoul-mask, a dinosaur of senility, and his whole
    body
A fungoid anemone of canker –

Can the caress of water ease him?
The flow will not let up for a minute.

What a change! From that covenant of polar light
To this shroud in a gutter!
What a death-in-life – to be his own spectre!
His living body become death's puppet!
Dolled by death in her crude paints and drapes
He haunts his own staring vigil
And suffers the subjection, and the dumbness,
And the humiliation of the role!

And that is how it is,
That is what is going on there, under the scrubby oak
    tree, hour after hour,
That is what the splendour of the sea has come down to,
And the eye of ravenous joy – king of infinite liberty
In the flashing expanse, the bloom of sea-life,

On the surge-ride of energy, weightless,
Body simply the armature of energy
In that earliest sea-freedom, the savage amazement of
    life,
The salt mouthful of actual existence
With strength like light –

Yet this was always with him. This was inscribed in his
     egg.
This chamber of horrors is also home.
He was probably hatched in this very, pool.

And this was the only mother he ever had, this uneasy
     channel of minnows
Under the mill-wall, with bicycle wheels, car tyres,
     bottles
And sunk sheets of corrugated iron.
People walking their dogs trail their evening shadows
     across him.
If boys see him they will try to kill him.

All this, too, is stitched into the torn richness,
The epic poise
That holds him so steady in his wounds, so loyal to his
     doom, so patient
In the machinery of heaven.

That Morning

We came where the salmon were so many
So steady, so spaced, so far-aimed
On their inner map, England could add

Only the sooty twilight of South Yorkshire
Hung with the drumming drift of Lancasters
Till the world had seemed capsizing slowly.

Solemn to stand there in the pollen light
Waist-deep in wild salmon swaying massed
As from the hand of God. There the body

Separated, golden and imperishable,
From its doubting thought – a spirit-beacon
Lit by the power of the salmon

That came on, came on, and kept on coming
As if we flew slowly, their formations
Lifting us toward some dazzle of blessing

One wrong thought might darken. As if the fallen
World and salmon were over. As if these
Were the imperishable fish

That had let the world pass away –

There, in a mauve light of drifted lupins,
They hung in the cupped hands of mountains

Made of tingling atoms. It had happened.
Then for a sign that we were where we were
Two gold bears came down and swam like men

Beside us. And dived like children.
And stood in deep water as on a throne
Eating pierced salmon off their talons.

So we found the end of our journey.

So we stood, alive in the river of light
Among the creatures of light, creatures of light.

Sources

The poems in this book were first published in the following
collections:

The Hawk in the Rain (Faber and Faber, 1957): The Jaguar; The
Horses; The Thought-Fox.
Lupercal (Faber and Faber, 1960): View of a Pig; Hawk Roosting;
Thrushes; An Otter.
Wodwo (Faber and Faber, 1967): Wodwo; The Bear; Gnat-Psalm;
Gog; Song of a Rat; The Howling of Wolves; Skylarks; Second
Glance at a Jaguar.
Season Songs (Faber and Faber, 1976): Swifts.
Moortown (Faber and Faber, 1979): from the sequence 'Adam and
the Sacred Nine': And the Falcon Came; The Skylark Came; The
Wild Duck; The Swift Comes the Swift; The Unknown Wren;
And Owl; The Dove Came. From the sequence 'Earth-Numb':
Tiger-Psalm; Night Arrival of Sea-Trout (also in *River*).
River (Faber and Faber, 1983): The Gulkana; The Merry Mink; An
August Salmon; An October Salmon; That Morning.
Wolfwatching (Faber and Faber, 1989): Wolfwatching; A Sparrow
Hawk; The Black Rhino; Little Whale Song; A Dove.
Uncollected: Bones.

Index of First Lines

Underwater eyes, an eel's 52
Upstream and downstream, the river's closed 41

We came where the salmon were so many 64
What am I? Nosing here, turning leaves over 1
What do they think of themselves 58
When the gnats dance at evening 7
With its effort hooked to the run, a swinging ladder 11
Woolly-bear white, the old wolf 2

Subject Index

This index refers readers to all four volumes of the *Collected Animal Poems*. Numbers in **bold** refer to volume numbers. Individual birds, fish and insects are listed under the category headings BIRDS, FISH and INSECTS.

black rhino 4:50
bull *see under* cow
bullfrog 3:111

calf *see under* cow
cat 1:50; 2:98
 kitten 3:7
cougar 1:68
cow 1:37; 2:15, 16, 18; 3:24, 36,
  49, 55, 61, 86, 116
 bull 3:61, 68
 calf 3:1, 24, 49, 86, 116
crab 1:12
 hermit 1:20

deer, roe 3:110
dog 2:97, 101
donkey 1:42; 2:48

elephant 1:82; 2:60
elk, Irish 3:72
ewe *see under* sheep

FISH:
 blenny 1:16
 brooktrout 1:55
 carp 2:87
 conger eel 1:4
 dab 1:53
 eel 3:92
 flounder 1:17
 loach 3:5, 21
 mackerel 3:8
 minnow 3:29
 pike 1:44; 3:11, 13, 53; 4:28
 salmon 3:73; 4:18, 41, 61, 64
 sea-trout 3:57; 4:55
 stickleback 1:34
 trout 3:21, 40; 4:41
foal *see under* horse

fox 1:38; 2:28, 40, 81, 103; 4:54
 Arctic 1:60
 vixen 2:80
frog *see* bullfrog

gander *see under* goose
goat 1:43; 2:71, 72, 74; 3:115
goose 2:29, 75, 78
 gander 2:40

hare 2:28, 89, 90, 91, 93, 95
 snow-shoe 1:56
hedgehog 2:88
hermit crab *see under* crab
horse 1:42; 2:20; 3:101; 4:32
 foal 2:11; 3:75
 pony 4:35
hyena 1:82

INSECTS:
 ant 1:58
 bee, honey 1:75; 2:51
 beetle 2:30
 blue-fly 3:89
 butterfly
  Red Admiral 1:31
  tortoiseshell 3:96
 caddis 3:48
 cranefly 3:84
 damselfly 3:70
 dragonfly 1:29
 flea 2:88
 fly 2:61, 63; 3:89
 gnat 4:7
 grasshopper 1:79
 honey bee 1:75; 2:51
 mayfly 3:94
 mosquito 3:14
 sandflea 1:6
 spider *see* spider

Irish elk *see* elk

jaguar 4:30, 56
jellyfish 1:13

kitten *see under* cat

lamb *see under* sheep
limpet 1:2
lion, mountain 3:95
lobster 1:5
lobworm *see under* worm

mermaid 1:1
mink 4:34
mole 1:41
moose 1:66
mountain lion 3:95
mouse 1:28; 2:58, 59
musk ox 1:70
mussel 1:21

octopus 1:15
otter 1:27; 4:52
ox, musk 1:70

pig 1:39; 2:41; 4:26
puma 1:68

rabbit 2:30
ragworm *see under* worm
ram *see under* sheep
rat 2:24, 29; 4:23

rhino, black 4:50

sea anemone 1:11
seal 1:22
sheep 1:32, 2:32, 33, 36; 3:15
  ewe 2:30; 3:45, 80
  lamb 2:31, 35, 36; 3:15,
    45, 80, 103
  ram 1:32, 2:30
shrew 1:49
shrimp 1:18
snail 1:26, 30
snow-shoe hare *see under* hare
spider 1:81; 3:30, 89
squirrel 1:46
starfish 1:10

tiger 3:109; 4:47
  tigress 3:9
toad 1:35

vixen *see under* fox
vole 2:29

weasel 2:56, 64, 84; 3:60
whale 1:3; 4:58
whelk 1:8
wolf 1:ix, 54, 64; 4:2, 39
wolverine 1:54
worm 1:25, 41; 2:83
  lobworm 2:111
  ragworm 1:14